UNICORNS

"Any book without a mistake in it has had too much money spent on it"

Sir William Collins, publisher

UNICORNS

NIGEL SUCKLING

ff&f

Unicorns

Published by
Facts, Figures & Fun, an imprint of
AAPPL Artists' and Photographers' Press Ltd.
Church farm House, Wisley, Surrey GU23 6QL
info@ffnf.co.uk www.ffnf.co.uk
info@aappl.com www.aappl.com

Sales and Distribution
UK and export: Turnaround Publisher Services Ltd.
orders@turnaround-uk.com
USA and Canada: Sterling Publishing Inc.
sales@sterlingpub.com
Australia & New Zealand: Peribo Pty.
michaelcoffey@peribo.com.au
South Africa: Trinity Books. trinity@iafrica.com

A catalogue record for this book is available from the
British Library.

ISBN 13: 9781 904 332 688
ISBN 10: 1 904 332 684

Design (contents and cover): Malcolm Couch
mal.couch@blueyonder.co.uk

Printed in China by Imago Publishing
info@imago.co.uk

CONTENTS

INTRODUCTION

O this is the creature that has never been.
They never knew it, yet none the less
Its motion, its bearing and slender neck,
Crowned by the gleam of its still gaze - they loved it.

Indeed it never 'was'. Yet because they loved it
A pure creature was born. They always left room.
And in that space, clear and void,
It raised its head lightly and scarce needed being.

They fed it no grain, but only
The wish that it might be.
And this gave the creature such strength,

That there grew from its brow a horn. Einhorn.
In its whiteness it drew near a virgin girl -
And was in the mirror's silver – and in her.

Rainer Maria Rilke (1875-1926) *The Unicorn*

Unicorn - - English
Licorne - - French
Einhorn - - German
Unicorno - - Italian
Unicornio - - Spanish
Qi Lin - - Chinese
Kirin - - Japanese

Unicorns are unique not just for their startling singular horns but because people carried on believing in them long after dragons, griffins, manticores and a host of other fanciful creatures had been consigned to myth and heraldry.

At the height of its fame in sixteenth century Europe a complete unicorn's horn was equal in value to a fair-sized town and most of the nobility carried at least a piece of one somewhere about them in the form of jewellery. The horn was also a popular component of jewelled drinking cups, cutlery and dinner table ornaments.

Apart from the unicorn's beauty, rarity and mystique – qualities we can readily identify with today – the main reason for its popularity was the then famous power of unicorn's horn to neutralise poison. It's forgotten how large a daily peril this was centuries ago, when food poisoning was both a popular tool of politics (think the Borgias) and a common hazard of poor domestic hygiene. Sudden death at the dinner table was all too frequent.

Besides being famous for preventing this, drinking or eating food touched by even a fragment of unicorn's horn was also believed to prolong life, libido and general well-being.

Queen Elizabeth I was presented with a narwhal tusk in 1577 by the explorer Martin Frobisher, who had picked it up on an island in Frobisher's Strait, northern Canada, while on his second search for the fabled North West Passage to the Pacific (during which he incidentally claimed Canada in Elizabeth's name). Whether or not he knew it was actually a narwhal tusk, it entered the Crown Jewels as the Horn of Windsor and was valued as a true unicorn's horn at between £10,000 and £40,000, well over a thousand times that by today's values.

Even at the time it was guessed that much of what passed for unicorn horn was fake. So, many tests were devised to prove the truth. When Elizabeth's successor King James I of England bought a complete horn for £10,000 he tried it by first giving a draught of poison to a servant, then a drink containing powdered unicorn horn as an antidote. When the unlucky servant died, James knew he had been tricked . . .

King James I was also responsible for the introduction of the famous unicorn into the British royal coat of arms in 1603. As King James VI of Scotland his arms had been supported by two unicorns, and the English ones by two lions. To symbolise his joint sovereignty over England and Scotland, one of each beast was thenceforth employed for the united realm.

In the seventeenth century powdered unicorn horn was a staple of the pricier apothecaries' shops because of its legendary curative powers, and it was valued at well over its weight in gold. Then word spread that most of the famous unicorn horns in circulation were in fact narwhal tusks, harvested off the Greenland coast.

The person who broke the secret was Danish zoologist Ole Wurm, who gave a public lecture in 1638 on narwhals and the true origin of most 'unicorn horns' in Europe. Not much immediate attention was paid, but the vital truth that Wurm released spread like a virus.

The kings of Denmark had grown rich for centuries by monopolising this trade and guarding its secret. Almost as a tease their coronation throne made around 1660 was a magnificent structure plated with 'unicorn' horn, and it was the envy of all the other European monarchs. It can be seen today at Castle Rosenberg near Copenhagen, home of the Danish Crown Jewels.

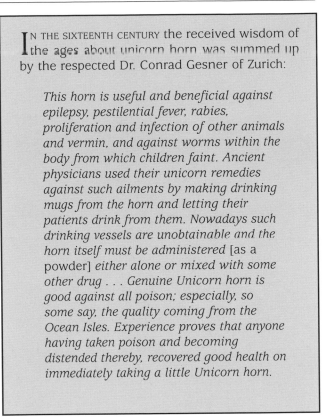

I N THE SIXTEENTH CENTURY the received wisdom of the ages about unicorn horn was summed up by the respected Dr. Conrad Gesner of Zurich:

> *This horn is useful and beneficial against epilepsy, pestilential fever, rabies, proliferation and infection of other animals and vermin, and against worms within the body from which children faint. Ancient physicians used their unicorn remedies against such ailments by making drinking mugs from the horn and letting their patients drink from them. Nowadays such drinking vessels are unobtainable and the horn itself must be administered* [as a powder] *either alone or mixed with some other drug . . . Genuine Unicorn horn is good against all poison; especially, so some say, the quality coming from the Ocean Isles. Experience proves that anyone having taken poison and becoming distended thereby, recovered good health on immediately taking a little Unicorn horn.*

Prices of unicorn horn plummeted towards the end of the seventeenth century. A complete horn belonging to Charles I in Britain fell in value from £8,000 in 1630 to just £600 in 1659, but the horn continued to be sold as a medicine for the next hundred years, and to be used as an emblem for European pharmacies for much longer – even down to the present when, for example, a pair of unicorns still adorn the entrance to the Apothecaries' Hall in

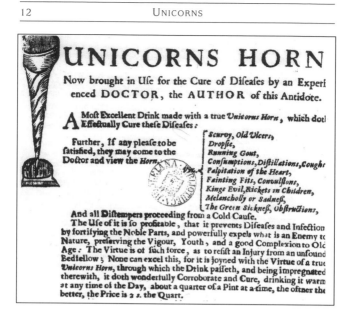

UNICORNS HORN

Now brought in Ufe for the Cure of Difeafes by an Experienced DOCTOR, the AUTHOR of this Antidote.

A Moft Excellent Drink made with a true *Unicorns Horn*, which doth Effectually Cure thefe Difeafes:

Further, If any pleafe to be fatisfied, they may come to the Doctor and view the Horn.

- *Scurvy, Old Ulcers,*
- *Dropfie,*
- *Running Gout,*
- *Confumptions, Diftillations, Coughs*
- *Palpitation of the Heart,*
- *Fainting Fits, Convulfions,*
- *Kings Evil, Rickets in Children,*
- *Melancholly or Sadnefs,*
- *The Green Sicknefs, Obftructions,*

And all Diftempers proceeding from a Cold Caufe.

The Ufe of it is fo profitable, that it prevents Difeafes and Infection by fortifying the Noble Parts, and powerfully expels what is an Enemy to Nature, preferving the Vigour, Youth, and a good Complexion to Old Age: The Virtue is of fuch force, as to refift an Injury from an unfound Bedfellow; None can excel this, for it is joyned with the Virtue of a true *Unicorns Horn*, through which the Drink paffeth, and being impregnated therewith, it doth wonderfully Corroborate and Cure, drinking it warm at any time of the Day, about a quarter of a Pint at a time, the oftner the better, the Price is 2 s. the Quart.

London and others still hang over chemists' shops scattered around Europe.

During the nineteenth century many acclaimed scientists applied their intellects to the question of the existence of unicorns, not least of them the celebrated French naturalist Baron Georges Leopold Cuvier, famous for his pioneering work on dinosaur fossils.

In a commentary on the description of unicorns in Pliny's *Natural History* Cuvier declared that in his opinion a cloven-hoofed ruminant, such as the unicorn was supposed to be, could not possibly have a single horn because it would have to grow over a division of the bone of its forehead. This and similar opinions carried the day in scientific circles and the rumours of unicorns that continued to come in from all corners of the world, particularly Africa and Asia, were dismissed as fanciful travellers' tales.

By the turn of the twentieth century the sceptics had mostly won the argument. Only a few romantics still dared suggest seriously (as in the famous case of Charles Gould in 1886, who even enlisted Darwin in support of his arguments) that unicorns had ever existed, at least not within the period that anyone had been writing about them.

Then in 1906, among a collection of exotic animals from Nepal presented to the Prince of Wales and intended for the London Zoo, there came a couple of indisputable unicorns – unicorn rams in fact, cloven-hoofed rams that were normal in every respect except that from each forehead there projected just a single horn . . .

CHAPTER ONE:
MYTHS & LEGENDS

ANCIENT AUTHORITIES

The earliest known reference to unicorns in classical literature is by Herodotus (484 – 425 BC) who mentions the existence of an Indian 'wild ass' with one horn, probably meaning the Indian rhino.

This was just a passing comment though. The first real description that sparked a thousand rumours was by the Greek historian Ctesias of Cnidas in the fourth century BC. He had been a doctor to Darius II and Artaxerxes II, emperors of Persia, for about seventeen years, during which time he amassed a wealth of travellers' tales about Persia, India and the Far East which he wrote down in his book *Persica* when he retired back to Greece.

This book inspired the young Alexander the Great to want to see the places for himself; which he famously did through conquering half of them.

Ctesias had no first hand experience of unicorns but recorded what he heard from people he believed reliable. He also probably handled a coloured drinking cup made from Indian rhinoceros horn which he was told had come from a unicorn. Although like all authors he must have hoped for fame, he almost certainly never guessed in his wildest dreams that his memoirs would help cause the collapse of his host empire and still be quoted over two thousand years later whenever unicorns are discussed.

THERE ARE in India certain wild asses which are as large as horses, and larger. Their bodies are white, their heads brown and their eyes dark blue. They have a horn on their forehead which is about a cubit long. The dust filed from this horn is administered in a potion as a protection against deadly drugs. The base of this horn, for some two hands' breadths above the brow, is pure white; the upper part is sharp and of a vivid crimson; and the remainder, or middle portion, is black. Those who drink out of these horns, made into drinking vessels, are not subject, they say, to convulsions or epilepsy. Indeed, they are immune even to poisons if, either before or after swallowing such, they drink wine, water or anything else from these beakers. [...] The animal is exceedingly swift and powerful so that no creature, neither the horse nor any other, can overtake it.

Alexander the Great's tutor Aristotle was sceptical about some of Cstesias's claims about unicorns but seems not to have questioned their existence. Aristotle reasoned that creatures with a solid hoof were more likely to have a single horn than those with cloven hooves, because solid hooves would leave less spare material in the creature's body for generating horns:

We have never seen an animal with a solid hoof and two horns, and there are only a few that have a solid hoof and one horn, as the Indian Ass and the Oryx.
Aristotle

Thanks to Aristotle's mistaken belief that the oryx naturally has a single horn, the idea spread wherever his works were read in places where there were no actual oryx to contradict him.

About a century after Cstesias another Greek called Megasthenes visited India and wrote a four volume description of the fabulous country which for centuries was the most complete account available in the West. In it he describes another kind of unicorn called a cartazoon (elsewhere known as a karkadann, cartazonon and many spellings in between) which had the feet of an elephant, the tail of a hog and a harsh bray. This would seem to be a rhinoceros except that he specifically describes the rhino elsewhere.

Almost certainly Megasthenes was just repeating two separate descriptions of the same animal without realising it because in Islamic tales the cartozoon or karkadann is basically the rhino, even when in art it has wings and looks something like a short-legged bull. Both his descriptions however came to be attached to the legend of the unicorn.

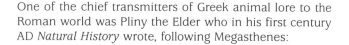

In Shatranj, the ancient Indian board game related to chess, the karkaddan piece is usually represented by a rhino head.

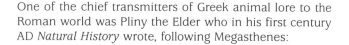

One of the chief transmitters of Greek animal lore to the Roman world was Pliny the Elder who in his first century AD *Natural History* wrote, following Megasthenes:

> *The fiercest animal is the Unicorn, which in the rest of the body resembles a horse, but in the head a stag, in the feet an elephant, and in the tail a boar, and has a deep bellow, and a single black horn three feet long projecting from the middle of the forehead. They say that it is impossible to capture this animal alive.*

Pliny also coined the term 'monoceros' which through the ages has been applied equally to the unicorn and the Indian rhino, adding to the confusion between them.

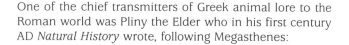

The other and probably more influential Roman scholar was Aelian whose encyclopedia *De Natura Animalium* repeated Cstesias and Megasthenes almost word for word in their often contradictory descriptions of the Indian 'Wild Ass' but added that India also produced horses with a single horn:

> *And from these horns they make drinking vessels, and if anyone puts a deadly poison in them and a man drinks, the plot will do him no harm. For it seems that the horn of both the horse and the ass is an antidote to the poison.*

This perhaps is one origin of the idea of the unicorn being a horned horse, though it is perhaps worth mentioning here with regard to ancient descriptions of animals that hippopotamus literally means 'river-horse', though a hippo no more resembles a horse than does a rhino.

Regarding the use of unicorn horns as drinking cups Aelian said: 'Only the great men use them after having them ringed with hoops of gold, exactly as they would put bracelets on some beautiful statue'. He also described of the unicorn's style of combat, using teeth and heels as well as its horn. The beast was said to defend itself so fiercely that in India the phrase 'hunting the unicorn' had become a proverb for chasing the impossible.

Aelian also had much to say about the astragalus, or ankle-bone of the unicorn. In the ancient world such bones from many creatures were widely used as both charms and dice and, in the unicorn's case, were valued almost as highly as the horn.

THE PHYSIOLOGUS

A quite separate channel by which knowledge of the unicorn entered Europe was the *Physiologus Graecae*, a compilation of natural lore written in Greek in Alexandria in the second or third century AD. For a while this book was second only to the Bible in popularity and was the foundation of most medieval bestiaries, however many other sources they drew upon.

The book derives its title from the many passages that begin 'The Natural Philosopher [or Physiologus] says . . .' This character was sometimes assumed to be Aristotle but was almost certainly an imaginary figure, a literary device for presenting the information.

Besides the unicorn, other fanciful creatures included among the descriptions of perfectly real ones (and there-fore also long assumed to be real) were the Gryphon, the Manticore and the Phoenix.

Copies of the book have survived in most languages of Europe and the Near East including Arabic, Coptic, Armenian, Georgian, Latin, French, German and Norse.

In his *Recensions of the Greek Physiologus* (1936) the Italian scholar Francesco Sbordone collated the contents of seventy-seven Greek manuscripts of the book ranging in length from twenty-seven to forty-eight chapters.

Isidore of Seville (c.560 – 636 AD) tried to clarify the physical distinction between the rhino and the unicorn in the bestiary section of his great encyclopaedia, but attributed the temperament of the rhino to the unicorn and so added to confusion between the two:

> *Rhinoceros in Greek means a horn in the nose. A Monoceros* [however] *is a Unicorn, and it is a right cruel beast. It has that name because it has in the middle of the forehead a horn four feet long. And*

that horn is so sharp and strong that he throws down all that he meets . . . And this beast fights often with the elephant and wounds, and sticks him in the womb and throws him down to the ground. The Unicorn is so strong that he cannot be taken by the might of hunters. But men that write of kind things say that if a maid is set, there he will come. And she opens her lap and the Unicorn lays thereon his head, and leaves all his fierceness and sleeps in that way: and he is taken as a beast without weapons and slain with the darts of hunters.

Although not mentioned in any of the early bestiaries, later ones sometimes tell of another way by which the unicorn can be captured. This is believed to have come from a description in a letter from Prester John to the Pope of how the lion sometimes overcomes the unicorn. Here is a translation of a lost Latin original:

[The Unicorn] *is an enemy to Lions, wherefore as soon as ever a Lion seeth a Unicorn, he runneth to a tree for succour, that so when the Unicorn maketh force at him, he may not only avoid his horn but also destroy him; for the Unicorn in the swiftness of his course runneth against a tree, wherein his sharp horn sticketh fast. Then when the Lion seeth the Unicorn fastened by the horn, without all danger he falleth upon him and killeth him.*

Edward Topsell *History of Four-Footed Beastes* 1607

In the bestiaries and folklore not just the lion but any decoy can use this trick to catch a unicorn, as shown in the Grimms' Fairytale *The Brave little Tailor*.

A LTHOUGH THE AUTHORS of *Physiologus* drew on other sources than Cstesias and Megasthenes – introducing the idea that the unicorn was a small creature that could be captured by virgins – they perpetuated the same confusion between the rhino and the unicorn. This confusion grew over the centuries as manuscripts were repeatedly copied and added to – as shown in these two separate extracts from a thirteenth century English bestiary:

> *The unicorn, which is also called monoceros in Greek, has this nature: it is a small beast not unlike a young goat, and extraordinarily swift. It has a horn in the middle of its brow and no*

hunter can catch it. But it can be caught in the following fashion: a girl who is a virgin is led to the place where it dwells, and is left there alone in the forest. As soon as the unicorn sees her, it leaps into her lap, embraces her and falls asleep there. Then the hunters capture it and display it in the king's palace.

The monoceros is a monster with a horrible bray. It has the body of a horse, the feet of an elephant and a tail like that of a stag. A horn of extraordinary splendour projects from the middle of its forehead, four feet in length, and so sharp that anything it strikes is easily pierced by the blow. It is never taken into the power of human beings while it lives. It can be killed but never captured alive.

The *Physiologus* also popularised another aspect of unicorn behaviour that passed into folklore and art as 'the Water Progidy' or 'the Water-conning Miracle'. One manuscript describes it like this:

There is a great lake in those regions where the animals gather to drink. However, before they assemble the serpent comes and spits venom into the water. The animals sense the poison and dare not drink, but await the coming of the unicorn. Up he comes, goes straight into the water and makes the sign of the cross with its

horn. This neutralises the venom. The unicorn sips some of the water and then all the other beasts too can drink.

Most versions of the *Physiologus* follow their descriptions of the beast with an allegory about its significance, as all beasts were assumed to have a moral purpose in the divine plan of Creation:

The unicorn signifies Christ, who was made incarnate in Mary's womb, was captured by the Jews, and was put to death. The unicorn's fierce wildness shows the inability of hell to hold Christ. The single horn represents the unity of God and Christ. The small size of the unicorn is a symbol of Christ's humility in becoming human.

THE BIBLICAL UNICORN

The third main channel by which the unicorn entered Western consciousness was the Bible. This was largely an accident of translation. In the third century BC King Ptolemy II of Egypt commissioned seventy (or seventy-two, according to some accounts) Jewish scholars to produce a Greek translation of the Old Testament in as many days, ensconcing them for the duration on the island of Pharos just off Alexandria. Known as the Septuagint, this was the basis of most subsequent translations of the Christian Bible.

When it came to translating the Hebrew word *re'em* the scholars were stumped. Clearly it referred to a wild and intractable beast, but which one? In the end they plumped for monoceros, probably thinking of the rhino, but in subsequent translations from the Greek this easily became 'unicorn' and thus entered the tongues of Europe with the full weight of divine authority behind it.

Most scholars now believe the *re'em* to have been a species of giant wild ox that died out in the region long before the Septuagint translation. Known as the aurochs or *bos primogenius*, fossils show ancient specimens up to ten feet tall at the shoulder, and up to fifteen feet in length, though in historical times they were closer to six feet tall at the shoulder. The various sub-species of this beast were the ancestors of all modern domestic cattle and the last true aurochs died out in Poland in the seventeenth century.

The only definite unicorn in the Bible is the one-horned goat that appeared in a vision to the prophet Daniel. In

IN THE King James Bible the unicorn is mentioned by name just seven times:

God brought them out of Egypt; he hath as it were the strength of an unicorn
Numbers 23:22, 24:8

His glory is like the firstling of his bullock, and his horns are like the horns of unicorns: with them he shall push the people together to the ends of the earth
Deuteronomy 33:17

Will the unicorn be willing to serve thee, or abide by thy crib? Canst though bind the unicorn with his band in the furrow? Or will he harrow the valleys after thee? Wilt thou trust him, because his strength is great? Or wilt thou leave thy labour to him? Wilt thou believe him, that he will bring home thy seed, and gather it into thy barn?
Job 39:9-12

Save me from the lion's mouth: for thou hast heard me from the horns of the unicorns
Psalms 22:22

The voice of the Lord breaketh the cedars; yea, the Lord breaketh the cedars of Lebanon. He maketh them also to skip like a calf; Lebanon and Syrion like a young unicorn
Psalms 29:5-6

For, lo, thine enemies, oh Lord, for, lo, thine enemies shall perish; all the workers of iniquity shall be scattered. But my horn shalt thou exalt like the horn of an unicorn: I shall be anointed with fresh oil
Psalms 92:9-10

And the unicorns shall come down with them, and the bullocks with the bulls; and their land shall be soaked with blood, and their dust made fat with fatness
Isaiah 34:7

the eighth chapter of his first book Daniel describes how in his vision he found himself in the palace at Susa in Persia by the river Ulai. Across the river he saw a great ram with two horns that ranged irresistibly to the north and west and south. Then from the west came charging another great ram with a single horn which attacked the first, broke its two horns and trampled it into the ground. For a while this unicorn ram reigned supreme, till its great horn broke and four smaller ones sprang up in its place.

An angel then explained the meaning of this dream to Daniel – that the first ram's two horns stood for the kings of Media and Persia, whose joint empire was then supreme in the region. The single horn of the second ram stood for the Greek king (Alexander the Great) who overthrew them, and the four smaller horns were the four kings who carved up his vast empire after Alexander's early demise – Ptolemy (Egypt), Seleucis (Persia), Antigonus (Greece and Macedonia) and Antiochus (the rest, including north-west India).

As the Book of Daniel was written well after Alexander's conquest of Persia, this episode is more a poetic description of events with the benefit of hindsight than true prophecy, but it still tells us much about the symbolism of animal horns at the time, and why a naturally single-horned beast would be held in special awe.

Alexander the Great was also sometimes shown on Greek coins as having ram's horns, from his Arabic nickname Zul-Qarnain (or Dhu'lquarnein) meaning 'Lord of Two Horns', showing that he was widely regarded as a living deity while in the world.

He was also known in Arabic as al-Sikandar or Iskandar.

In India his story mingled or possibly evolved into the legends of Skanda, the elegant and ever-youthful pan-Indian war god who is often pictured with a ram.

THE CHRISTIAN UNICORN

While the Bible gave credibility to the unicorn and told that it was a wild and intractable beast, it offered very little else in the way of description. That was left to the folk traditions that grew around the various literary fragments.

Because of its association with virgins the unicorn naturally became a symbol for Christ, and gave rise to the complex allegory of the Unicorn Hunt as seen in glorious medieval tapestries, most especially those in the Cloisters, Metropolitan Museum of Art in New York. This aspect was strengthened by the legend of the unicorn dispelling poison and snakes from the drinking pool to make it safe for other creatures, which was seen as a parallel in nature of Christ's work of redemption in dispelling the lies of Satan.

On a quite opposite tack, the legendary fierceness of the

James of Viraggio, Archbishop of Genoa in the thirteenth century, published a collection of parables called *The Golden Legend*. One was a widely popular tale now believed to have been adapted from a Buddhist parable in India, where the preacher Barlaam was revered as a Christian saint. Almost certainly the unicorn in the tale was originally meant to be an Indian rhino, but through the usual confusion it entered Western folklore as a classic unicorn:

> *Once there was a saint named Barlaam who lived in the desert near Senaah and who often preached against the illusory pleasure of the world.*
>
> *Thus he spoke of a man fleeing in haste from a Unicorn who would devour him. Falling into a well, he happened to catch hold of a bush but failed to find a proper foothold. With the raging unicorn glaring down on him from the rim of the well, he caught sight of a dreadful fiery dragon waiting with open maw for him to drop. From the narrow ledge on which he was teetering, four serpents distend their fangs. A pair of mice, one black and the other white, gnaw away at the roots of the bush to which he is clinging, while the bush itself is about to break off. But as he lifts his eyes, he spots honey dripping from the branches of the bush and, forgetting all about his peril, he surrenders himself fully to the sweetness of the honey.*
>
> *The unicorn, as Barlaam expounded in his parable, was death which pursues man every-*

where. The well was the world filled with every evil. The bush was human life finally extinguished by the steady erosion of day and night, represented by the mice. The four serpents stand for the human body composed of the four elements which must disintegrate if they become disturbed. The dragon is the bottomless pit of hell threatening to swallow up mankind. But honey is the worldly pleasure to which man surrenders, forgetting all peril.

Old Testament unicorn led to it sometimes being used in homilies as a figure of Satan. A bestiary long attributed to St Basil of Caesarea (330 - 379 AD) was one of the first to take this line. Quoting Psalm 22, in which David prays to be saved from the mouths of lions and the horns of unicorns, he continues:

> *The unicorn is evilly inclined towards man. It pursues him and when it catches him it pierces him with its horn and devours him . . . so take care, O Man, to protect thyself from the Unicorn, that is to say from the Devil. For he plotteth evil against man and is skilled in doing him harm.*

Although there is no mention of unicorns in Genesis, in the late middle ages it became common to show a unicorn or two with Adam and Eve in the Garden of Eden. Where they are naming the animals the unicorn is usually first in line, and when they were expelled from Eden the unicorn was often said to have accompanied them into the world to share and relieve their sorrows.

Although many old illustrations show the unicorn leading the other beasts onto Noah's Ark, a quite contradictory notion about the unicorn is that it did not in fact survive the Flood at all, either (depending on the source) through pride in refusing to join the other beasts, disruptive behaviour on the Ark, or simply because it was too big – as suggested by the Talmud comment that the *re'em* was 'as large as a mountain'.

All the beasts obeyed Noah when he invited them into the ark, all but the unicorn confident of his strength he boasted: 'I shall swim!' For forty days and forty nights the rains poured and the oceans boiled as in a pot and all the heights were drowned. The birds of the air clung onto the ark and when the ark pitched they were all engulfed. But the unicorn kept on swimming. However, when the birds emerged again they perched on his horn and he drowned − and that is why there are no more unicorns today!

Ukrainian folk tale

CHAPTER TWO:
UNICORNS
IN THE EAST

The first rumours of unicorns came from the Middle East and India but very different ideas about the creatures developed in the East and West. While in the Far East a quite independent idea of the unicorn developed which, while curiously similar in some ways, is very different in others.

Japan has its own unicorn based on the Chinese one, but it has almost been forgotten and the image that comes into most minds there today is the snow-white, graceful creature from European tapestries.

TRAVELLERS' TALES

In the sixth century AD an Alexandrian traveller known as Cosmas Indicopleustes (or 'The Indian Sailor' because of his long travels there) retired to a Nestorian monastery on Mt Sinai to write his memoirs, which he called *Christian Topography*. The book was largely devoted to refuting ideas about the world that seemed to contradict the Scriptures, but Cosmas also wrote enthusiastically about what he had seen and heard on his travels, including an illustrated section on exotic animals. The rhino he had to describe at second hand, only having seen one from a great distance. He depicts it as having two horns on its nose, one behind the other, as has the African rhino (as opposed to the Indian rhino which has only one horn) but muddies the waters by showing it as otherwise closely resembling a horse.

But he was on slightly firmer ground with the unicorn:

THE MONOCEROS OR UNICORN
This animal is called the unicorn. I cannot say that I have seen him, but I have seen four brazen figures of him set up in the four-towered palace of the King of Ethiopia. From these figures I have been able to draw him as you see. They speak of him as a terrible beast and quite invincible, and say that all his strength lies in his horn. When he finds himself pursued by many hunters and on the point of being caught, he springs up to the top of some precipice whence he throws himself down and in the descent turns a somersault so that the horn sustains all the shock of the fall, and he escapes unhurt.

Ethiopia was the home of the legendary Prester John (or Presbyter John, because he was a priest-king), the

Orthodox Christian ruler who claimed descent from Solomon and the Queen of Sheba, and who counted the Ark of the Covenant among his treasures.

Ethiopians claim that they still have the Ark, housed in the Church of our Lady Mary of Zion in Axum. Only its

appointed guardian is allowed to see it however, and he is not allowed to leave its sanctuary once appointed, except in a coffin.

In Persia there were rumours of another kind of unicorn – the *shadhahvar*. This was supposed to be an antelope with a single hollow, branched horn that made sweet music in the wind. When other animals were drawn to the pleasant sound it would kill them.

In 1389 a Dutch priest, Johannes van Hesse of Utrecht, claimed to have seen the unicorn's famous Water Prodigy for himself while on pilgrimage to Palestine. When his account was published a century later it had enormous influence because it was assumed that the testament of a priest on pilgrimage must be true, but it has since been questioned whether he ever even left his home town:

Near the field Helyon in the Promised Land is the river Marah, whose bitter waters Moses made sweet with a stroke from his staff and the children of Israel drank thereof. To this day, it is said, malicious animals poison this water after sundown, so that none can thereupon drink any longer from the stream. But early in the morning, as soon as the sun rises, a unicorn comes out of the ocean, dips his horn into the stream and drives out the venom from it so that the other animals may drink thereof during the day. This, as I describe it, I saw with my own eyes.

Johannes van Hesse

In 1503 a traveller from Bologna named Lewis Vartoman (Ludovico Barthema) published a popular account of his travels in the Middle East. Among the many marvels he describes in his *Itinerary* were two unicorns he heard about in the temple at Mecca, gifts from the Emperor of Ethiopia. The creatures were:

. . . shown to the people for a miracle, and not without reason for their rarity and strange nature. The one of them, which is much higher than the other, yet not unlike to a colt of thirty months of age, in the forehead grows only one horn, in manner right forward, of the length of three cubits . . . This beast is of the colour of a horse of weasel colour, and has a head like a hart, but no long neck, a thin mane hanging only on the one side. Their legs are thin and slender, like a fawn or a hind. The hooves of the fore feet are divided in two, much like the feet of a goat. The outward part of the hind feet is very full of hair. This beast doubtless seems fierce and wild, but tempers that fierceness with a certain comeliness.

A NOTHER FAMOUS and far more trustworthy witness of the unicorn in the Holy Land was Friar Felix Faber who visited it with several other respectable travellers in 1483. His illustrated account was published by the Dutch artist and printer Erhard Reuwich, who was with the group. On route from Jerusalem to Cairo via Mt Sinai they stopped for a rest in the mountains one day when:

> *Towards noon we spotted an animal gazing down at us from a mountain peak. We thought it was a camel and wondered how a camel might remain alive in the wilderness, and this speculation raised a discussion among us as to whether there might also be forest camels. Our guide Kalin approached us, however, and stated that the animal must certainly be a rhinoceros or a unicorn, and he pointed out to us the single horn which jutted from the animal's forehead. With great caution we gazed back at this most noble creature, regretting that it was no closer for us to examine it still more minutely . . . We rested for some time at the bottom of the mountain where the animal stood regarding us as pleasantly as we regarded it, for it stood still and moved not until we had gone on our way.*

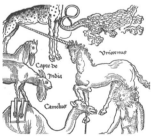

At first hand Vartoman also saw in the port of Zeila in Somalia some cattle with single horns. Similar one-horned cattle were also seen by later travellers in East Africa who learned that the Bantu produced them artificially by manipulating the horns.

A nineteenth century encyclopaedia, drawing on old travellers' tales, said a Bantu was:

> . . . never content to leave the horns as they are. He will cause one horn to project forward and the other backward. Now and then an ox is seen in which a most singular effect has been produced. As the horns of the young ox sprout they are trained over the forehead until the points meet. They are then manipulated so as to make them coalesce, and to shoot upwards from the middle of the forehead, like the horn of the fabled unicorn.

John G Wood *Natural History of Man*, 1868

A while after Vartoman around 1590 the English adventurer Edward Webbe, famous for his tall stories, wrote:

> I have seen in a place like a park adjoining Prester John's court, three score and seventeen unicorns and elephants all alive at one time, and they were so tame that I have played with them as one would play with young lambs.

Ambroise Pare, a sixteenth century army doctor who published diaries of his travels, was sceptical about the existence of unicorns, despite their mention in the Bible. However, he was open-minded enough to record the testimony of a fellow doctor, Louis Paradis, who claimed to have seen one in Alexandria, where it had been sent as a gift to the Great Moghul from Prester John.

Paradis described the unicorn as being about the size of a boar-hound with a glossy, dark coat, a slender neck and a foot long horn between the ears. The head was thin and short but the eyes large and wild. The legs were thin and tipped by cloven hooves. Paradis was told by the Ethiopians who had brought it that there were many other unicorns in their country, but they were so wild they were hard to catch.

Another late sixteenth century traveller who wrote about unicorns was Marmol Caravajal, who spent over twenty years in North Africa, eight as an Arab prisoner of war. In his *General Description of Africa* (1573) he wrote, probably repeating what he had read or heard rather than as a witness:

> *Among the Mountains of the Moon in High Ethiopia there is found a beast called a unicorn which is as large as a colt of two years, and of the same general shape as one. Its colour is ashen and it has a mane and a large beard like that of a he-goat; on its brow it has a smooth white horn of the colour of ivory two cubits long and adorned with handsome grooves that run from base to point. This horn is used against poison, and people say that the other animals wait until this one comes and dips its horn in the water before they will drink. It is such a clever beast and so swift that there is no way of killing it.*

FAR EASTERN LEGENDS

Marco Polo (1254-1324) on his travels in the Far East had his illusions about unicorns shattered by an encounter with rhinos in Java, describing them as:

> . . . *scarcely smaller than elephants. They have the hair of a buffalo and feet like an elephant's. They have a single large black horn in the middle of the forehead . . . They spend their time by preference wallowing in mud and slime. They are very ugly brutes to look at. They are not at all such as we describe unicorns when we relate that they let themselves be captured by virgins, but clean contrary to our notions.*

Despite his unflattering comments, Marco Polo's description encouraged the first European visitors to North America to look for them there, especially while it was still believed that America was in fact the eastern tip of Asia. Many claimed to have found unicorns, or at least to have heard about them from the native Americans.

India was the source of many rumours of unicorns that reached the West but they were never held in quite the same esteem there, even when not being confused with the rhino, or being used as parables of restrained power. There are some instances though, when unicorns are credited or associated with a mystical agenda.

Legend tells that when the Buddha delivered his famous sermon at Benares a unicorn gazelle came and knelt at his feet to listen. Its single horn was seen as a symbol of Nirvana.

A Buddhist hymn uses the unicorn as a model of behaviour:

In the Province of Aqaus [in Ethiopia] *has been seen the Unicorn, that Beast so much talked of and so little known; the prodigious Swiftness with which this Creature runs from one Wood into another has given me no Opportunity of examining it particularly, yet I have had so near a sight of it as to be able to give some Description of it. The Shape is the same as that of a beautiful Horse, exact and nicely proportioned, of a Bay Colour, with a black Tail, which in some Provinces is long, in others very short; some have long Manes hanging to the Ground. They are so Timorous that they never Feed but surrounded with other Beasts that defend them.*

Hieronymous Lobo
A voyage to Abyssinia
trans. Samuel Johnson 1735

Free everywhere and at odds with none
Content with what comes your way
Enduring peril without alarm,
Fare solitary as the Unicorn
Like a lion fearless of the howling pack
Like the breeze ne'er trapped in a snare
Like the lotus unsoiled by its stagnant pool,
Fare solitary as the Unicorn

In the Indian Ramayana (I; 9-10), Mahabharata (III, 110-113) and many other sources is told the curious tale of a human unicorn – the hermit boy Rishyashringa who had a single gazelle horn growing out of his forehead.

The story goes that there was once a great sage named Vibhandaka who dwelt in the forests of Madhya Pradesh, in an area now known as the Chandal Valley. Vibhandaka was so powerful that often he had only to think a thing for it to become so. And in some way connected with this power a she-gazelle that attended the sage conceived and gave birth to his son. He was human in every way, except that from his forehead projected a single gazelle horn.

The boy was given the name Rishyashringa, meaning 'deer-horn', and he became a hermit with his father. So sheltered was their life that he grew to be a young man without ever meeting a woman or girl, or even learning of their existence.

Meanwhile his fame as a saint spread far and wide, for it was said that the boy was so holy that flowers sprang up where he trod and all creatures flourished in his company. His fame travelled till it reached the ears of Lompada, Rajah of the kingdom of Anga where a drought was threatening to destroy the harvests and half the people. The king's advisors told him if only he could persuade the young saint to come to the capital, the drought would be broken.

Well, the Rajah sent messengers with this invitation but they returned empty handed, saying that he had only smiled at them until they had gone away. The Rajah then sent soldiers to bring him by force, but they too returned empty handed, saying they could not bring themselves to lay hands on such a saint. Then the king's daughter stood forward and said that she would fetch the hermit to the palace.

So she travelled – some say alone, some say with other maids – till she came to the forest. Never having seen a beautiful maid before, Rishyashringa thought Shanta must be an angel from heaven. Strange urges and longings woke in his breast and loins for the first time and soon he fell completely under the spell of her charms. When Shanta brought the hermit meekly to her father's palace the drought did indeed break and the land was saved. Rishyashringa then married his princess and by all accounts they lived happily ever after.

Some scholars see in the story of Rishyashringa an echo of the *Physiologus* story of the virgin capture of the unicorn, but it is currently impossible to know which came first.

According to Ssanang Ssetzen, in the year 1206 Genghis Khan invaded northern India with a vast army. Then as he led the way through the final pass and saw the rich plains of India spread out below, like a banquet for the taking, a beast with one horn came up and bowed humbly three times before the Khan. Genghis was so struck by this that he was thoughtfully silent a long while. At last he said:

> *This middle kingdom of India before us is the place, men say, in which the sublime Buddha and the Bodhisattvas and many powerful princes of old time were born. What may it mean that this speechless wild animal bows before me like a man? Is it that the spirit of my father would send me a warning out of heaven?*

Whereupon he turned his army around and marched away.

Tibet has many traditions about unicorns. A famous traveller, Abbe Huc, wrote in the account of his visit to Tibet in the 1840s:

> *The Unicorn, which has long been regarded as a fabulous creature, really exists in Tibet. You find it frequently represented in the sculptures and paintings of the Buddhist temples. Even in China you often see it in the landscapes that ornament the inns of the Northern provinces. We had for a long time a small Mongol treatise on Natural History, for the use of children, in which a Unicorn formed one of the pictorial illustrations. The Chinese Itinerary says, on the subject of the lake you see before your arrival at Atzder (going from east to west), "The Unicorn, a very curious animal, is found in the vicinity of this lake, which is forty Li long."*

Many European travellers fully expected to find the legendary unicorn alive and well in Tibet, without ever quite doing so; although Hodgson (who gave his name to Hodgson's Antelope) is supposed to have acquired the skin of a unicorn that had died in the King of Nepal's zoo and sent it to Calcutta.

But nowhere in the Far East did the unicorn win such reverence as in China where even today in some regions the highest compliment is to tell someone that a unicorn must have smiled on their birth.

In the Taoist tradition the unicorn was one of the four most fortunate beasts who emerged from the cosmic egg with the creator, Pan Gu (or Pan Ku) and helped him shape the universe. The others were the dragon, the tortoise and the phoenix.

When after 18,000 years Pan Gu had finished separating the sky from the earth, he died. His breath became the wind and clouds, his eyes became the sun and moon. His stomach, head and limbs became the chief mountain of the world, watered by the rivers of his sweat and tears; his flesh became the fertile soil and his hair the plants and trees which took root in it. The fleas on his body became the human race. The four most fortunate beasts dispersed into the world and multiplied.

The Chinese unicorn is called the Qi Lin. Like the Western unicorn it is shy and elusive and credited with wisdom and gentleness. Unlike the Western unicorn it has no hint of a fierce side to its nature and there is only one known mention of it being white. It was said to show itself at the

birth and death of great rulers or sages, and so traditionally images of the unicorn were hung around the bed of
expectant mothers, or on flags at weddings.

The ancient *Book of Rights* describes the Qi Lin as:

> *Chief among four-footed beasts. It resembles the
> stag but is larger. It has a single horn, the tip of
> which is fleshy, indicating that it is not used in
> battle. There are five colours in the hair of its back
> - red, yellow, blue, white and black - and the hair of
> its belly is dark yellow. It does not tread any living
> grass underfoot nor eat any living creature.*

The *Shu Qing* adds:

> *Its call in the middle part is like a monastery bell.
> Its pace is regular. It rambles on selected grounds
> and only after it has examined the locality. It will
> not live in herds or be accompanied in its move-
> ments. It cannot be beguiled into pitfalls or captured
> in snares.*

A Qi Lin is recorded as appearing to the legendary
Emperor Fu Xi around 3,000 BC and revealing to him the
secret of writing by means of enigmatic signs on its back.
The reigns of his four successors were also marked by the
appearance of unicorns, and the period was looked back
on as a Golden Age of peace, justice and sound govern-
ment.

The last of the Five Emperors was Shun and his chief
minister of justice was Kao yao. The minister's judgements were so famously wise that he was given the Qi Lin
as his emblem. Kao yao is also said in the histories to have

often been helped by a unicorn in his judgements. When he could not decide the case, this unicorn was brought out and it would indicate with its horn if the suspect was guilty, a judgement that could result in their execution.

Whether the beast was a true Qi Lin is doubtful. Some accounts suggest a unicorn ram or goat.

When the legendary Yellow Emperors were succeeded by lesser mortals, the Qi Lin was seen more and more rarely, though everyone watched out eagerly for them whenever the throne changed hands. But in the chaotic sixth century BC the birth of Confucius, China's greatest sage, was heralded by a unicorn that appeared to his mother and dropped a jade tablet in her path bearing the inscription: 'The son of the mountain crystal, the essence of water, will redeem the fallen kingdom of Chu and become a King without a crown'.

Towards the end of his life as Confucius was writing his *Spring and Autumn Annals* a strange beast was reportedly killed by accident nearby. Going to see for himself, Confucius recognised it as a Qi Lin and read it as a portent of his own demise. Drawing his book to a hurried end, he laid down his pen and did no more serious writing until his death a few years later.

Four centuries later a pure white Qi Lin was seen in royal palace park by the Emperor Wu ti of the Han dynasty. Wu ti added a viewing gallery to the palace in hopes of seeing it again but it was to be the last time a true unicorn gave its blessing to a Chinese ruler.

The Qi Lin was not forgotten however, and people continued to look out eagerly for them with each new Emperor. Then in the fifteenth century during the reign of the Ming Emperor, Yung Lo, a wild rumour spread that a Qi Lin had again come to the palace as a gift from the Rajah of Bengal. It was in fact a giraffe but despite its obvious differences from the legendary unicorn, the euphoria continued until the Emperor set the tone by installing it in the Imperial Zoo with no special distinction from the other exotic beasts there.

In Japan the native unicorn is known as the Kirin and is very similar to the Chinese one, but has largely been forgotten. There is a popular brand of Japanese beer called Kirin with a clear picture of the beast on its label but few recognise it for what it is and commonly suppose that the word means a giraffe.

CHAPTER THREE:

UNICORNS IN HISTORY

ANCIENT TALES

Besides garbled rumours of the one-horned rhino of India, another quite likely source of tales of the agile, goat-like unicorn of the Near East are the Ibex and Oryx, both of which when seen in profile from a distance (as is often the case when they are keeping a wary eye on passing humans) can seem to have just one horn. Occasionally they even do, when one has broken off in battle.

Many small bronze Persian statues of unicorn ibexes have survived from the second century BC. Their purpose is unknown but they quite likely helped convince visitors that the ibex was naturally one-horned, or at least that this was common.

The *Elasmotherium* or woolly rhino is another possible candidate for some European rumours of unicorns. The creature is generally believed to have died out in prehistoric times but just possibly survived long enough to be remembered in legend. Almost cer-

tain though, is the occasional discovery as the Ice Age ended of
bodies of the woolly rhino preserved in ice which would have
generated rumours of its continued
existence, as with the discovery of
dinosaur bones and the legends of
dragons in China.

While broadly resembling the
modern rhino, the *Elasmotherium*
was larger, had longer legs and a
very much larger horn mounted
almost between the eyes.

However, an inescapable contribution to the legends and
descriptions of the mythical unicorn of course comes
from its surly and uncouth alter ego, the Indian rhino
(*Rhinoceros unicornis*), with which since ancient times it
has always been confused and whose horn in many parts
of the world, even today, has almost as potent a reputation that is largely responsible for its near-extinction.

The Indian rhino is the only one with a single horn. It
lives in forests when possible and spends much time
wallowing in mud to prevent skin infestations. It can swim
and, although slow to get moving, can run at up to thirty-
five miles per hour for short bursts. It has keen senses of
hearing and smell but very poor eyesight.

Its momentum and poor eyesight may well have
suggested the trick of unicorn capture in which its prey
runs straight for a tree and then dodges behind it at the
last moment.

It is a mostly solitary creature except at watering
holes and when breeding. After mating, the male rhino
leaves the female to tend their offspring for up to two
years

A NOTHER CAUSE of all the rumours of unicorns is their occasional appearance as freaks of nature. The earliest record of this is in Plutarch's *Life of Pericles* where he writes that the head of a unicorn ram was sent to the tyrant from one of his farms. This was read (correctly as it happens) as an omen of his victory in a current political battle.

> *There is a story, that once Pericles had brought to him from a country farm of his a ram's head with one horn, and that Lampon, the diviner, upon seeing the horn grow strong and solid out of the midst of the forehead, gave it as his judgment, that, there being at that time two potent factions, parties, or interests in the city, the one of Thucydides and the other of Pericles, the government would come about to that one of them in whose ground or estate this token or indication of fate had shown itself.*

Plutarch

By a strange coincidence Pericles himself suffered from a curious backwards elongation of the skull that led to most portraits showing him wearing a helmet to hide it. Satirists made great fun of this deformity and Athenian poets called him Schinocephalos, or squill-head (the squill being a maritime onion).

Julius Caesar in his history of the Gallic Wars describes a kind of unicorn he was told existed in the vast Hercynian Forest of Germany:

> *There is an ox of the shape of a stag, between whose ears a horn rises from the middle of the forehead, higher and straighter than those horns which are known to us. From the top of this, branches, like palms, stretch out a considerable distance. The shape of the female and of the male is the same; the appearance and the size of the horns is the same.*

THE AGE OF ENLIGHTENMENT

In the sixteenth and seventeenth centuries the forerunners of modern museums were the 'cabinets of curiosities' assembled by travellers, wealthy dilettantes and scientists to display the marvels of the world. Two famous modern collections which started this way are the Pitt Rivers collection in Oxford, England, and the Museum of Jurassic Technology in Los Angeles, California.

One famous cabinet was assembled by Ole Wurm, the Danish zoologist who blew the whistle on the trade in narwhal tusks as unicorn horns.

Typical of their contents is this extract from a catalogue of the one at the Kensington castle of Sir Walter Cope:

> *. . . holy relics from a Spanish ship; earthen pitchers and porcelain from China; a Madonna made of feathers, a chain made of monkey teeth, stone shears, a back-scratcher, and a canoe with paddles,*

all from India; a Javanese costume, Arabian coats; the horn and tail of a rhinoceros, the horn of a bull seal, a round horn that had grown on an Englishwoman's forehead, a unicorn's tail; the baubles and bells of Henry VIII's fool, the Turkish emperor's golden seal . . .

Some cabinets had a more serious intent though. One of the most celebrated of all was that of Ulysse Aldrovandi (1522-1605), founder of the botanical gardens in Bologna and widely recognised as one of the fathers of modern Natural History. His collection housed over 18,000 exhibits and was one of the wonders of the age.

His partial catalogue *Monstrorum Historia* (published posthumously like most of his writings in 1642) included a curious account of a contemporary human unicorn from northern France. This was Frantz Trouilli who lived in the forests near Lille. He came to the attention of the wider world through a certain gentleman named Laverdin who was in the habit of hunting in the forests. One day while addressing a group of peasants he noticed that one of them would not raise his hat, as was the feudal custom. When it was forcibly removed, it was to reveal a ram-like horn growing from the poor man's right forehead.

Laverdin sent Trouilli to the French king, who happened to be nearby and from there he was taken to Paris and shown as a curiosity seen by many. Apparently the horn had not begun growing until he was about seven years old and he was in all other respects quite normally healthy.

In 1663 great interest was stirred by the apparent discovery of a fossilised unicorn in a gypsum sink hole at Quedlinburg, Germany. This was examined by the prominent scientist Otto von Guericke (most famous today for his vacuum experiment with the Magdeburg hemispheres, and the invention of the first real electricity generator) who produced a curious reconstruction of a unicorn with no apparent hind legs.

About a hundred years later a similar skeleton was found nearby at Scharzfeld in the Einhornhohle (Unicorn Cave).

The philosopher Leibniz examined both skeletons in 1749 and declared that they had convinced him of the reality of unicorns, something which he had previously doubted. Both skeletons were subsequently lost.

PT Barnum for a while exhibited what he claimed to be the skeleton of a unicorn, though it is unknown whether it was one of the Harz skeletons.

The Harz Mountains have a long association with unicorns and many other mysteries. Embraced by the ancient Hercynian Forest, they were possibly responsible for the tale of unicorns that reached Caesar's ears.

The cave near Scharzfeld was called the Unicorn Cave long before the eighteenth century discovery there. It is said to have acquired its name this way:

Long ago, around the time Christianity first came to the region, a wise woman lived close by in another cave called the Steingrotte. People came to her from miles around for advice and healing, which roused the anger of the local monks. They persuaded the Frankish king to lend them some soldiers who were led by one of the monks to capture the witch.

They found her, but as they closed in a unicorn emerged from some trees and she climbed on its back and escaped. They gave chase but the soldiers were weighed down by their arms. The monk raced lightly ahead and they saw the witch suddenly stop and turn her unicorn to face him. She waved her hands in the air and the monk suddenly disappeared. The wise woman rode off and when the soldiers arrived panting at the scene they found a shaft leading down to a cave, on whose floor the monk lay shattered and dead. So they named it the Unicorn Cave.

A unicorn is still the emblem of Scharzfeld and the Einhornehohle is its major tourist attraction.

Bones and even stalactites from this and other caves nearby were a major source of 'fossil unicorn horn' which European apothecaries sold alongside what they believed the real thing, and which was judged almost as effective a panacea.

The Harz horns are now reckoned to have mostly come from cave bears, mammoths and other ice age animals, but stalactites and even fossilised tree branches were also passed off as 'fossil unicorn horn'.

One of the sceptics who helped bring an end to the lucrative pharmaceutical trade in 'unicorn horn' of all kinds, and to expose the true origin of all the most famous horns in Europe, was Sir Thomas Browne who in *Pseudodoxia Epidemica* (III:xxiii) 1646 wrote, after an attack on the trade in 'fossil unicorn':

> *The like deceit may be practised in the teeth of other Sea-animals; in the teeth also of the Hippopotamus or great Animal which frequenteth the River Nilus: For we read that the same was anciently used instead of Ivory or Elephants tooth. Nor is it to be omitted, what hath been formerly suspected, but now confirmed by Olaus Wormius, and Thomas Bartholinus and others, that those long Horns preserved as precious rarities in many places, are but the teeth of Narhwales; to be found about Island* [Iceland], *Greenland, and other Northern regions; of many feet long, commonly wreathed, very deeply fastened in the upper jaw, and standing directly forward, graphically described in Bartholinus, according unto one sent from a Bishop of Island, not sep-*

arated from the cranium. Hereof Mercator hath taken notice in his description of Island: some relations hereof there seem to be in Purchase, who also delivereth that the horn at Windsor, was in his second voyage brought hither by Frobisher. These before the Northern discoveries, as unknown rarities, were carried by Merchants into all parts of Europe; and though found on the Sea-shore, were

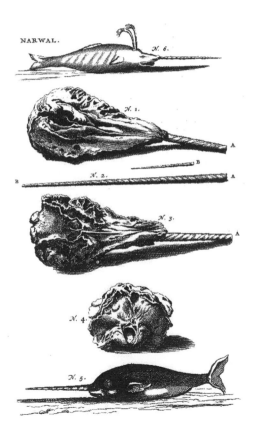

NARWAL.

sold at very high rates; but are now become more common, and probably in time will prove of little esteem; and the bargain of Julius the third be accounted a very hard one, who stuck not to give many thousand crowns for one.

The revelation from scientists that what people had been buying as unicorn horn was mostly, if not all, fake (and that the most revered horns came from the sea- and not land-unicorn) did not immediately collapse the market because all horns were then considered to have therapeutic virtues, as is still widely believed in Africa, China and elsewhere today. Unicorn horn just happened to be considered the most potent of all.

It had long been known that there were fakes. A French traveller Andre Thevet reported seeing, around 1550, islanders in the Red Sea straightening walrus tusks for export to East and West as true unicorn horn.

Richard Hakluyt, an English geographer, recorded that a doctor friend from Bristol had shown him a walrus tusk collected in the St Lawrence Gulf and said that he had: 'made tryall of it in ministering as medecine to his patients, and had found it as soveraigne against poyson as any Unicornes horne'.

So, exposing the truth about unicorn horn did not immediately collapse its price. It took time for word to spread and then the fall in value was quite steep and dramatic over the next fifty years or so till it was no more valuable than other horns used in medicine. It was only finally almost extinguished when science put an end to the medicinal use of horns altogether in the eighteenth century.

SEA UNICORN

In 1994 a beautifully carved 'unicorn's horn' was auctioned at Christie's in London for nearly half a million pounds. As reported in the London *Times*, the seller had picked it up for £12 in 1957 as part of a bundle of walking sticks at a sale of the contents of a house in the Cathedral Close in Hereford. It was assumed that it had once been one of the Cathedral's treasures. Since then other cathedrals have been taking much better care of theirs . . .

David Ekserdjian, head of Christie's sculpture department, gave his first impressions of the Hereford horn:

It was wrapped up in a newspaper inside a cardboard tube, but the minute I held it in my hand I knew I was in the presence of a great and extraordinary object. There was something about its weight and heft, as well as the sheer beauty of its carving. It has an almost tangible power, something you can feel coursing through your veins.

The horn was intricately carved in the twelfth century with human figures, foliage, dragons and other fantastic creatures. It is now in the care of the World Museum, Liverpool.

The horn was of course, like most other famous Medieval unicorn horns, a narwhal tusk.

The narwhal (*Monodon monoceros*) is one of the rarest whales in the world, with a population estimated between 10,000 and 40,000. It lives in Arctic waters between Canada, Greenland and Russia

and its body resembles that of the beluga whale, to which it is related.

The name 'narwhal' comes from the Old Norse word *náhvalr* meaning 'corpse whale', probably because of the creature's colouring and/or its habit of floating upside down on the surface. Although a protected species narwhals are still hunted legally by the Inuit of Canada and the tusks can fetch several thousand dollars each on the open market, depending on the length and condition.

In Inuit legend the narwhal came into being when a woman tied to the rope of a hunter's spear was dragged into the sea when he harpooned a beluga whale, and the two became inextricably tangled.

Narwhals are mottled white and brown in colour, with dark backs and pale bellies. Females give birth after a gestation period of fifteen months. Little is known about their behaviour in the wild, beyond that they live in family groups and hunt collectively, mainly feeding on fish, shrimp and squid. They can dive up to 1000 metres and stay underwater for about twenty minutes.

The famous horn is in fact a tusk, a left front tooth that has become enormously elongated to up to ten feet (3 m). Usually this just occurs in the males, but females also occasionally develop a thin tusk, and the males very occasionally have two.

There is no certainty about the tusk's purpose. Once it was assumed to be used to break ice to reach the air (like all whales, narwhals have to surface to breathe). Then it was popularly thought to serve mainly as a duelling weapon to warn off other males and attract mates, but closer study has shown that while the males do rub tusks in a kind of ritual jousting, it seems more of a game or form of communication than a battle.

Recent findings of a complex nerve structure within the hollow tusk suggest that it may be a sensory organ. Dr Martin Nweeia, a dentist, Harvard professor and marine animal researcher at the Smithsonian Institution examined two narwhal tusks with an electron microscope and found millions of tiny tubes connecting the nerve at the core of the tooth with its surface. Nweeia and his colleagues believe these could enable the narwhal to sense changes in temperature, pressure and even the salinity or mineral content of the sea. Nweea is part of the multinational Narwhal Tusk Research project established in 2000 to investigate the phenomenon.

The narwhal tusk is the only non-curving one in nature, also the only one that grows in a spiral. It is also flexible and can yield as much as a foot in an eight-foot length without breaking. While most mammal teeth are soft on the inside and hard on the outside, the narwhal tusk is just the reverse, contributing to its flexibility.

The Inuit name for the narwhal means: "he who points to the sky" because of the creature's frequent habit of raising its head out of the water with the tusk pointing straight up, as if testing the wind.

AMERICAN UNICORNS

As Canada was the true home of the most treasured European unicorn horns, it is fitting that the earliest settlers there were quite convinced of the existence of true unicorns in the area where eastern Canada and the United states now meet. Desceliers' map of 1542 shows unicorns in the region between Quebec and Maine, and his later maps repeated this.

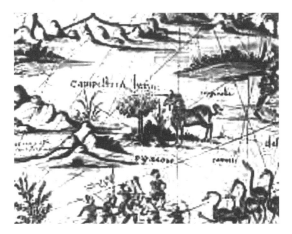

In a natural history by John Ogilby (*America* 1671, based on a Dutch work by Arnoldus Montanus) the unicorn is listed matter-of-factly alongside the moose, beaver and American eagle, its reality being taken for granted in the area between New York and Canada.

The unicorn was also included in a natural history by Louis Nicolas, a missionary in what was then New France from 1664 to 1674. To a description of the beast he added the comment: 'Few of them are killed by the Indians because they are rare, their young die easily, being hyper-sensitive as to their diet'. Although not claiming to have seen the unicorn for himself, Nicolas was convinced of their reality by the many travellers in America who claimed to have seen them, from the conquistadors on.

For instance Friar Marcus of Nizza, who set out from Mexico in 1539 to find the legendary Seven Cities of Cibola, had written that on arrival he was shown, among other wonders: 'a hide half as big again as that of an ox and told it was the skin of a beast which had but one horn upon its forehead, bending towards its breast, and that out of the same goeth a point forward with which he breaks any thing that he runs against'.

Sir John Hawkins, in the journal of his voyage of 1564, wrote that in Florida:

> *The Floridians have pieces of Unicorns' horns, which they call Souanamma, which they wear about their necks, whereof the Frenchmen obtained many pieces. Of those Unicorns they have many; for they affirm a beast with one horn which, coming to the river to drink, puts the same in the water before he drinks. Of this Unicorn's horn there are some of our company that, having got them of the Frenchmen, brought them home to show.*

Possibly the most influential early account though is that of Dr Olfert Dapper in *Die Unbekante Neue Welt*, 1673, where with an accompanying illustration he confidently stated (quite probably, like John Ogilby, drawing his information from Arnoldus Montanus):

On the Canadian border there are sometimes seen animals resembling horses but with cloven hooves, rough manes, a long straight horn upon its forehead, a curled tail like that of the wild boar, black eyes and a neck like that of the stag. They live in the loneliest wildernesses and are so shy that the males do not even pasture with the females except in the season of rut, when they are not so wild. As soon as this season is past, however, they fight not only with other beasts but even with their own kind.

HERALDRY

The science of heraldry has faithfully preserved to modern times various phases of some of those remarkable legends which . . . exhibit the process whereby the greater part of mythology has come into existence. Thus we find the solar gryphon, the solar phoenix – a demi-eagle displayed issuing from flames of fire – the solar lion and the lunar unicorn,

which two latter noble creatures now harmoniously support the royal arms. I propose in the following pages to examine the myth of the unicorn, the wild, white, fierce, chaste moon, whose two horns, unlike those of mortal creatures, are indissolubly twisted into one; the creature that endlessly fights with the lion to gain the crown or summit of heaven, which neither may retain, and whose brilliant horn drives away the darkness and evil of the night.

Robert Brown *The Unicorn: a Mythological Investigation* London 1881

In heraldry the unicorn represents extreme courage, virtue and strength.

Although there are some isolated examples from earlier, it was only in the fifteenth century that the unicorn's popularity really took off as a heraldic emblem across Europe. Probably this was because earlier its reputation had been tainted by suggestions of its occasional wild and uncontrolled savagery – its identity with Satan rather than Christ. By the fifteenth century this had slipped into the background behind the creature's virtues. The savagery is just hinted at by the chains worn by most heraldic unicorns, showing that the savage side of their natures had been tamed.

The unicorn was probably first adopted for the royal coat of arms of Scotland around the end of the fourteenth century by King Robert I or II, as shown by the arms carved around this time over the gateway of Rothesay Castle, Bute, a favourite residence of Robert II. A rival theory is that it was first introduced as one supporter of the arms by James I of Scotland (1424-1437), replacing a dragon. Then in 1503 James IV adopted two unicorns, which continued until the union of England and Scotland, when James VI of Scotland succeeded Queen Elizabeth to become James I of England in 1603.

Partly to symbolise the union of the two old enemies, King James introduced the unicorn as one supporter of the British coat of arms in a pair with the English lion. More than this though, James wrote that because of the unicorn's traditional association with the moon, and the lion's with the sun, the pairing symbolised a balancing of fundamental forces of nature:

> *The Lion-sun flies from the rising*
> *Unicorn-moon and hides behind the*
> *Tree or Grove of the Underworld;*
> *The Moon pursues, and, sinking in*
> *Her turn, is sun slain.*

Unicorn coins were the first native gold coinage in Scotland and were minted from around 1484 to 1525. Because of their attractive and original design they were popular gifts from Scottish kings to visiting ambassadors. The front shows a unicorn holding a shield bearing the Scottish Lion emblem while the back bears a radiant sun or star imposed on a cross.

In 2004 the British Royal Mint issued a collector's set (i.e. non-negotiable) of pound coins bearing designs submitted but not used for new issues of the everyday currency. Four designs representing each of the four countries of the United Kingdom were minted on the reverse. The one representing Scotland was a unicorn, thus almost commemorating its illustrious ancestor.

HMS UNICORN

Linking an age when most people still believed in unicorns, not yet having felt the tide of scepticism spreading from the ivory towers, to one in which the reverse is probably true, is the aptly named wooden frigate HMS Unicorn.

One of the longest serving ships in the British Royal Navy it was built in Chatham Dockyards, Kent, and launched in 1824. She was one of the last of the successful Leda class of ships modelled on the design of a French vessel, the Hebe, captured in 1782.

The Unicorn frigate is the second oldest ship afloat in Britain, and probably the best preserved and least altered wooden hull in the world. This is largely thanks to having had a sheltered existence. Being launched in a time of relative peace, she was immediately mothballed and did not see any action at all until the 1850s when lent for a few years to the War Department to serve as a powder hulk at

Woolwich, after which she was again laid up at Sheerness – made obsolete by the rise of steam power.

Finally in 1873 the Unicorn sailed to Dundee for conversion into a drill ship for the Royal Naval Reserve. In both World Wars the ship also served as Area Headquarters of the Senior Naval Officer, Dundee.

This quiet existence meant that in 1939 another Navy ship came to be named HMS Unicorn without anyone realizing at first that the name was already in use. This was an aircraft carrier built in Belfast. The confusion caused by having two HMS Unicorns led to the wooden frigate's name being changed for as long as the aircraft carrier was active.

The second HMS Unicorn won battle honours in the Atlantic, Norway and the Mediterranean. Then from 1950-53 she served in the Korean War. The aircraft carrier was scrapped in 1959, after which its wartime captain's widow ceremonially restored its name to the frigate in Dundee.

The HMS Unicorn was finally decommissioned in September 1968 and saved from being scrapped by the Unicorn Preservation Society. Today it is a major Dundee tourist attraction.

The oldest commissioned warship of all, not just in Britain but the world, is Nelson's Victory in dry dock at Portsmouth, which although open to visitors, is still officially the flagship of the Royal Navy in commemoration of the century-defining victory at Trafalgar.

CHAPTER FOUR

THE UNICORN IN ART

The saintly hermit, halfway through his prayers
stopped suddenly, and raised his eyes to behold
the unbelievable: for there before him stood
the legendary creature, startling white, that
had approached soundlessly, pleading with his eyes.

The legs, so delicately formed, balanced a
body wrought of finest ivory. And as
he moved, his coat shone like reflected moonlight.
High on his forehead rose the magical horn, the sign
of his uniqueness: a tower held upright
by his alert yet gentle, timid gait.

The mouth of softest tints of rose and grey, when
opened slightly, revealed his gleaming teeth,
whiter than snow. The nostrils quivered faintly:
he sought to quench his thirst, to rest and find repose.
His eyes looked far beyond the saint's enclosure,
reflecting vistas and events long vanished,
and closed the circle of this ancient mystic legend.

Rainer Maria Rilke (1875 – 1926) *The Unicorn*

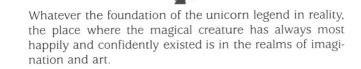

Whatever the foundation of the unicorn legend in reality, the place where the magical creature has always most happily and confidently existed is in the realms of imagination and art.

The unicorn embodies an ideal that teases us with the possibility of its being real, while remaining just beyond the bounds of being proved either way because, as we have seen, some unicorns have existed from time to time. It is a dream creature, but one that hints that it might just be real if the universe were just a little bit closer to perfection. It is not wildly fantastic like the wyvern or the hippogriff, just a slight step removed from the everyday.

One of the earliest places where the unicorn entered conscious fiction was in the great cycle of French romances that built up around Alexander the Great in the Middle Ages, just as they did around Arthur of Britain.

In the Bible Alexander the Great (356-323 BC) is represented by the unicorn ram in Daniel's vision of the palace of Susa, but he has many other associations with unicorns in the tales of both Europe and the Middle East.

Alexander's famously wild horse Bucephalus (Ox-head), which he tamed at the age of thirteen and rode into many of his greatest battles, is often illustrated as a uni-corn in the romances. In Islamic art Alexander is also often shown hunting or riding unicorns.

It's also perhaps relevant that in both history and leg-end when Bucephalus died Alexander's success also came to an end. His troops rebelled against further conquests in India and a large proportion died during their return to Persia. Alexander himself soon died as well, of suspected poisoning.

Whether a unicorn or not, whether coincidence or not, Alexander's fate was tied in with that of Bucephalus, something he seemed to recognise at the time through the lavish care given to the beast, which often travelled in its own coach on long marches.

In the *Song of Alexander* written by Pfaffen Lamprecht in the twelfth century we hear of a gift from Queen Candace to Alexander, a gem even more precious than the horn itself and found at its base:

> *I had from this most wealthy queen*
> *A beast of proud and noble mien*
> *That bears in his brow the ruby-stone*

> *And yields himself to maids alone.*
> *But few such Unicorns are found*
> *On this or any other ground,*
> *And only such are ever captured*
> *As pure virgins have enraptured.*
> *No man yet of woman born*
> *Endures the terror of his horn.*

In Wolfram von Eschenbach's *Parzival*, the stone is mentioned as one of the remedies applied to the Grail King's wounds (in vain as it happens, since nothing but the attainment of the Grail can do that):

> *We caught the beast called Unicorn*
> *That knows and loves a maiden best*
> *And falls asleep upon her breast;*
> *We took from underneath his horn*
> *The splendid male carbuncle stone*
> *Sparkling against the white skull-bone.*

Albertus Magnus, alchemist and one of the most influential thinkers of the Middle Ages, believed this precious stone or 'male carbuncle' to be the king of gems, able to dispel poison, guard from plague and banish sadness, evil thoughts and nightmares. He said it could be employed as either an amulet or a powder and a good stone would shine so brightly of its own accord as to be visible through clothing.

The unicorn caught the imagination of other alchemists in the days when their study was still more an art than a science. In the rare sixteenth century *Book of Lambspring* (analysed by C.G. Jung in his eleven year grapple with alchemical symbolism) is a series of symbolic images or 'emblems' of psychic states the alchemist was likely to encounter on his dream quest for the Philosopher's Stone, together with their interpretations.

The third engraving is of a deer and Unicorn standing together in a forest. Under the heading HEAR WITHOUT TERROR THAT IN THE FOREST ARE HIDDEN A DEER AND AN UNICORN the caption reads:

> *The sages say truly that two animals are in this forest; one glorious, beautiful and swift, a great and strong deer; the other a Unicorn. If we apply the parable of our art, we shall call the forest the body. The Unicorn will be the spirit at all times. The deer desires no other name but that of the soul. He that knows how to tame and master them by art, to couple them together and to lead them in and out of the forest, may justly be called a Master.*

THE UNICORN LADY AND THE KNIGHT OF THE LION

One of the most popular romances of the fourteenth century was the ballad *The Unicorn Lady and the Knight of the Lion*. The Unicorn Lady was the daughter of the King of Friesland. She was so graceful and pure that a unicorn came to live with her. In time she married a brave knight but, as was the custom of the day, this did not prevent her attracting many platonic lovers who went questing for adventures in her name, and with her husband's blessing.

Chief of these suitors was the penniless but bold Knight of the Lion, so called because of the lion that became his constant companion. All went well till a wicked noble with designs on the Unicorn Lady brought news to her that her champion the Knight of the Lion had perished. She collapses and is kidnapped and carried off to the wicked one's castle.

At the same time, someone tells the Knight of the Lion that his lady is dead and he falls into madness for a time. Finally he learns the truth and in a rage he storms the kidnapper's castle, rescues the lady and side by side, on the backs of their respective beasts, they ride away and she is restored to her husband.

This tale possibly helped inspire the famous Lady of the Unicorn tapestries in the Cluny Museum, Paris, woven around 1490. They are in no way direct illustrations but what they do have in common is that the tapestries show the lion and unicorn in harmony, instead of their usual combat. The tapestries illustrate the senses of sight, taste, hearing, smell and touch, plus the virtue of dedication.

Tracey Chevalier's bestselling 2003 novel *The Lady and the Unicorn* weaves a lively and convincing tale around the creation of these tapestries, which also inspired poet Rainer Maria Rilke to write about unicorns.

The other most famous unicorn tapestries are the Unicorn Hunt series of seven in the Cloisters Gallery of the Metropolitan Museum of Art in New York. The twelve foot high tapestries tell in gloriously colourful detail of the start of the hunt; finding the unicorn by a fountain where it is purifying the water with its horn for the other beasts to drink; two tapestries then show the hunt itself, with the unicorn defending itself boldly though surrounded by spears and dogs; then the unicorn is lured and made defenceless by a maiden in a garden; but she cannot save him because in the sixth tapestry we see the unicorn first speared and then carried apparently dead on horseback to the royal palace. Then in a clear allegory of Christ in the final tapestry we see the unicorn alive and whole again, still bleeding slightly but tamely resting beneath a pomegranate tree in a fenced garden, lightly tethered to the tree. The wild unicorn has been tamed.

The tapestries are believed to have been woven in Brussels to French designs around 1500. They disappeared during the French Revolution, only surfacing again in the 1850s when six of them were found on a farm being used to shield vegetables from frost.

They were bought in 1922 and donated to the Metropolitan Museum by John D Rockefeller. In 1936 the seventh tapestry showing the maiden capture was found in France and reunited with the rest, though in damaged fragments.

KING ARTHUR
AND THE UNICORN

As we have seen, the unicorn was a popular emblem for medieval knights, especially after the fifteenth century, when it had come to embody all the highest ideals of chivalry.

But while unicorns were common in the romances about Alexander the Great, they are curiously rare in the parallel cycle of Arthurian stories. Many other fantastic creatures show – the Questing Beast, dragons, giants, lions and magical deer, but barely a unicorn.

A rare exception comes at the end of the fourteenth century fable of the Knight of the Parrot (*Le Chevalier Papegau*, first edited and published by Ferdinand Heuckenkamp 1896).

In *Le Chevalier Papegau* the story tells how in his youth King Arthur went off sailing alone in search of adventure. A wild storm stranded him on a strange shore with no sign of habitation save for a single square, red tower with no windows or doors. Seeking shelter, Arthur calls and calls till finally a man's head appears over the battlements. He's friendly enough but says he can't offer Arthur any help till his son comes home.

While they wait
Arthur hears his new
companion's tale, called
down from the top of
the walls. It turns out
that he is a dwarf who
had once served as a
jester to the King of
Northumbria. Then one
day he had gone too
far, offended the King
and been banished
with his wife to this
deserted shore. She
had died in childbirth
soon after and, while
searching in the woods

for some shelter for his new-born son, the dwarf had
stumbled upon a nest of unicorn fawns. Well, he was so
surprised that he dropped the baby. Then the unicorn
mother appeared and chased him into the woods.

After he had escaped and then realised about his
missing baby, the dwarf crept back and saw the child
feeding at the unicorn's breast along with her fawns. Well,
in short that was how the child was weaned; and thanks
to the magical properties of the unicorn's milk he grew to
be a giant and she became his inseparable companion
after her own offspring had grown and left. In fact, the
dwarf concluded, she was with him now out hunting for
their dinner.

Just as the dwarf finished his tale the ground began to
tremble and the proof of it came striding towards them –
a giant with a tree trunk for a club on his shoulders, and
at his heels came trotting a dainty unicorn.

In the Welsh Mabinogion tale of Peredur (Perceval or
Parsifal) the forfeit he has to pay for losing a magic gam-

ing board is to slay a unicorn. The Dark Maid setting the task describes the beast as:

> A stag, swift as the swiftest bird, and there is one horn in its forehead the length of a spear-shaft, and it is as sharp of point as aught sharpest-pointed. And it browses the tops of the trees and what herbage there is in the forest. And it kills every animal it finds therein. And those it does not kill, die of hunger. And worse than that, it comes every night and drains the fish pond in its drinking, and leaves the fish exposed, and most of them die before water comes thereto again.

Peredur tracks down the unicorn and, when it charges him, ducks aside and strikes off its head with a sword. Then another lady comes along on horseback and rebukes him for having slain: 'The fairest jewel that was in my dominion.'

Peredur, being bound by an oath or *geisa* to obey every woman he meets, then has to pay another forfeit before he can go on his way. The question of which female was telling the truth about the unicorn is left unresolved.

In the early seventeenth century Honore d'Urfe's popular and influential pastoral romance *Astrea* centred on a Spring of True Love guarded by lions and unicorns. When at the end the lovers are attacked by lions, they are rescued by the unicorns, but when the dust settles over the battle all the beasts have turned to stone and the lovers lie seemingly dead. Luckily Cupid steps in to revive them and provide a happy ending.

In another Romantic novel *The Magic Horn* by Achim von Arims a young farmer sings of his dairymaid lover:

With sunbeams dazzling my pursuers
Like a unicorn free do I bound
Till even, away from my tortures
To virgin's lap escape I've found
To catch me with gossamer she knew
But with the dawn she set me free
On her lashes gazed I true
But those sweet eyes she shut on me

Lo! In the mute, mid wilderness,
What wondrous Creature? – of no kind! –
His burning lair doth largely press –
Gaze fixt – and feeding on the wind?

From his stately forehead springs
Piercing to heaven, a radiant horn, –
Lo! The compeer of lion-kings!
The steed self-armed, the Unicorn!

Ever heard of, never seen,
With a main of sands between
Him and approach; his lonely pride
To course his arid arena wide,

Free as the hurricane, or lie here
Lord of his couch as his career! –
Wherefore should this foot profane
His sanctuary, still domain?

Let me turn, ere eye so bland
Perchance be fire-shot, like heaven's brand,
To wither my boldness! Northward now,
Behind the white star on his brow
Glittering straight against the sun,
Far athwart his lair I run.

George Darley (1795 – 1846) *The Unicorn*

Leonardo da Vinci (1452 – 1519) wrote a bestiary, probably as a playful exercise, in which he drew a curious contrast between the temperaments of the unicorn and camel:

TEMPERANCE
The camel is the most lustful animal that there is, and it will follow the female a thousand miles, but if it lived continually with its mother or sister it would never touch them, so well does it know how to control itself.

INTEMPERANCE
The unicorn through its lack of temperance, and because it does not know how to control itself for the delight that it has for young maidens, forgets its ferocity and wildness; and laying aside all fear goes up to the seated maiden and goes to sleep in her lap, and in this way the hunters take it.

IN THE Grimms' Fairytale about the Brave Little Tailor a King tries to dispose of the hero by setting him impossible tasks, starting with the slaying of two giants that have been terrorising the land and rashly promising the tailor half the kingdom and his daughter's hand in marriage if he succeeds. Well, the wily tailor disposed of the giants by climbing a tree above their heads while they slept and tossing rocks at them, so each giant thought the other was doing it. Then in the fight that followed (egged on by timely rocks thrown from above) they ended up killing each other in their rage.

Then the Tailor demanded his reward of the King, who regretted his rash promises, despite relief at the giants' death, and thought of a new plan to shake off the hero. 'Before I can give you my daughter and half of my kingdom,' said he, 'you must first rid us of another menace to our realm because we'll have no peace until then. In the forest there lives a unicorn that kills everyone it meets. Catch the beast and bring him to me, and then you can have your reward.'

'I'm less frightened of a unicorn than two giants!' said the Tailor coolly and, gathering a rope and an axe, he set off gaily towards the forest with a troop of the King's soldiers. Once there he told his reluctant companions to wait on the outskirts and went on in alone. It did not take long for the unicorn to scent him and circle around, looking for an opening to charge.

'Steady! Steady!' cried the Tailor. 'You're not going to have me that easily'. He lined himself up carefully and when the beast charged he ran for all he was worth and when it was right on his heels, thundering and screaming like a steam train, the Tailor sprang nimbly behind the tree he was aiming for. The unicorn, too slow to turn, ran straight into the tree and its horn rammed deep into the trunk and stuck fast.

'Now I have you,' cried the Tailor; and with much care, he came back, tied up the unicorn with his rope and then cut the horn free with his axe. Then he led the hobbled creature in triumph out of the woods and back to the palace to claim his reward and the hand of his princess.

THE LION AND THE UNICORN

With a few exceptions, the unicorn and lion are legendarily hostile towards each other. This dates back to ancient times and Babylonian carvings that show their combat.

The Lion and the Unicorn
Were fighting for the crown
The Lion beat the Unicorn
All around the town
Some gave them white bread,
Some gave them brown,
Some gave them plum cake
And drummed them out of town

The old English nursery rhyme is often presumed to recall the ancient enmity between England and Scotland, and certainly that symbolism helped its survival in the English language, but it almost certainly long predates those countries' union and even the wars that went before.

Symbolically the lion and unicorn stand for polar opposites like sun and moon, male and female or yin and yang. So there is a natural inclination towards conflict even though it is pointless for either side to seriously try and win. They represent complementary qualities and as in the Chinese philosophy behind yin and yang, actual conflict is a failure of wisdom, a sign of imbalance.

The unicorn's identity with the moon is not as obvious as the lion's with the sun, as shown in astrology and elsewhere, but is clear enough from the creature's silver-white colouring and affinity with mirrors. Its horn is also identified with the crescent moon.

An old Middle Eastern legend tells how at the dawn of time the lion and unicorn chased each other across the heavens. For fourteen years the lion chased the unicorn, steadily gaining upon it, but the unicorn dodged around the lion and for the next fourteen years the chase was reversed. When the unicorn had almost caught the lion, it ducked behind the World Tree and the unicorn impaled itself in the trunk and was devoured.

This chase came to be re-enacted in the course of the lunar month, for half of which the sun chases the moon across the sky, and for half the reverse. Usually it is the moon that dies and must be reborn but just occasionally, when there is a solar eclipse, the unicorn briefly triumphs.

The scene of the lion and unicorn clashing by the tree (usually shown as a palm tree) appears on ancient

Assyrian cylinder seals and is echoed in all forms of art right through to the Middle Ages. By some unknown chain of circumstances one half of the scenario came to appear on a drinking horn in the treasury of York Minster, which is carved in Middle Eastern style and possibly even came from there, though it was most probably made in southern Italy.

This is the Horn of Ulph, an eleventh century drinking vessel traditionally said to have been given to the Minster by a Viking chieftan named Ulph Thoroldsson as a token of some land in the North Riding he was donating, and

which is still known in the Cathedral deeds as the *Terrae Ulphi*. The story goes that Ulph had got so fed up with his sons disputing their inheritance that he gave it all to the church instead, symbolically draining his favourite wine-cup in one flourish and laying it on the altar.

Lewis Carroll took up the theme light-heartedly in *Through the Looking Glass* where Alice meets the unicorn and lion as they rested from their great battle. After being introduced to the unicorn she then met his opponent:

> *The Lion had joined them while this was going on. He looked very tired and sleepy, and his eyes were half shut. "What's this!" he said, blinking lazily at Alice, and speaking in a deep hollow tone that sounded like the tolling of a great bell.*

> *"Ah, what is it now?" the Unicorn cried eagerly. "You'll never guess! I couldn't."*

The Lion looked at Alice wearily. "Are you animal – or vegetable – or mineral?" he said, yawning at every other word.

"It's a fabulous monster!" the Unicorn cried out, before Alice could reply.

"Then hand round the plum-cake, Monster," the Lion said, lying down and putting his chin on his paws.

T.H. White in his *Once and Future King* tells how Morgause, the less talented but equally witchy sister of Morgan le Fay, once led a couple of visiting knights on a unicorn hunt. Her virginity being but a faint memory, the plan naturally failed so her grown sons, eager to win her approval, set out on a hunt of their own. Recruiting a kitchen maid who really was still a virgin, they set their trap and the unicorn duly came and knelt before her . . .

In modern fantasy fiction the unicorn surfaces in many popular books such as the Harry Potter series, C.S.Lewis's *The Last Battle*, Anne McCaffrey's *Acorna* series and Terry Brooks' *The Black Unicorn*, to name just a few – but most popular of all with enthusiasts is the cult classic *The Last Unicorn* by Peter S Beagle. Since first publication in 1968 it has never been out of print and has consistently headed the favourites list of both unicorn enthusiasts and fans of general fantasy, having sold over five million copies and been translated into over twenty languages.

The story opens with the eponymous unicorn learning that she is the last one left in the world, and setting out with the clueless aspiring wizard Schmendrick to find out what has become of the rest . . .

The novel was made into an animated film in 1982, scripted by Beagle and directed by Jules Bass and Arthur

Unicorn with bursting heart
Breath of love has drawn:
On his desolate crags apart,
At rumour of dawn,

Has blared aloud his pride
This long age mute,
Lurched his horn from side to side,
Lunged with his foot.

'Like a storm of sand I run
Breaking the desert's boundaries,
I go in hiding from the sun
In thick shade of trees.

'Straight was the track I took
Across the plains, but here with briar
And mire the tangled alleys crook,
Baulking desire.

'O there, what glinted white?
(A bough still shakes.)
What was it darted from my sight
Through the forest brakes?

'Where are you fled from me?
I pursue, you fade;
I run, you hide from me
In the dark glade.

'Towering high the trees grow,
The grass grows thick.
Where you are I do not know,
You run so quick.'

Robert Graves *The Unicorn and the White Doe*

Rankin. Among the actors voicing the parts were Mia Farrow, Alan Arkin, Christopher Lee, Angela Lansbury, Jeff Bridges and Tammy Grimes. The soundtrack was by Jimmy Webb.

Probably the most popular non-animated film for unicorn lovers is Ridley Scott's 1985 *Legend* starring Tom Cruise, Mia Sara and Tim Curry. A unicorn also plays a significant role in Ridley Scott's cult *Blade Runner*, based on a story by Philip K Dick, where it appears in the dreams of the hero Deckard as a hint that he may not actually be the normal human being he assumes he is.

To see how popular the unicorn currently is in literature, try typing the word into the search engine of your favourite online bookstore and skim through the results. Children's books and fantasy dominate the list but there are some interesting entries outside those categories.

CHAPTER FIVE:

THE UNICORN TODAY

MAN-MADE UNICORNS

Great excitement and controversy broke out at the London Zoological Gardens in 1906 at the exhibition of two unicorn rams, part of a gift of exotic animals from the King of Nepal to the Prince of Wales:

> *Although receiving the name of unicorn-sheep, these animals really possessed a pair of horns, for if we examine one of their skulls and remove the horn-sheath from its bony support it will be noticed that the latter is composed of two quite separate structures.*

Berridge *Marvels of the Animal World*, 1921

During the controversy the British Resident at the Nepalese Court wrote:

> *There is no special breed of one-horned sheep in Nepal, nor are the specimens which have been brought here for sale natural freaks. By certain mal-treatment ordinary two-horned sheep are converted into a one-horned variety. The process adopted is branding with a red-hot iron the male lambs when about two or three months old on their horns when*

they are beginning to sprout. The wounds are treated with a mixture of oil and soot and when they heal, instead of growing at their usual places and spreading, come out as one from the middle of the skull . . . I am told that the object of producing these curiosities is to obtain fancy prices for them from the wealthy people of Nepal.

Inspired by background knowledge of this, in 1933 biologist Dr W Franklin Dove of Maine University decided to test the rumours of artificial unicorns for himself after realising that horns do not grow out of the skull. They begin as loosely attached bits of tissue under the skin, which then root themselves into the bone. So in theory they could sprout anywhere on the head, even over a division of bone in the forehead.

Taking a day-old Ayreshire bull calf, Dove surgically removed its horn buds, trimmed them to fit together and replanted them in the centre of its forehead. Within three months the young bull had a single straight, solid horn over a foot long. This horn later easily made it the leader of its herd and proved a useful tool for uprooting fences.

On 7 February 1984 Timothy G Zell patented (US Patent #4429685) a surgical procedure for producing unicorn goats, based on Dr Dove's experiment. In the patent Zell claimed that positioning the horn over a goat's pineal gland stimulated the creature's spiritual and mental powers. Four of his unicorn goats were for a while exhibited by the Ringling Brothers and Barnum & Bailey Circus in the US, including one called Lancelot the Living Unicorn.

In April 1985 US federal inspectors ruled that the Circus was not entitled to bill the creatures as 'unicorns'.

THE CELESTIAL UNICORN

The one true unicorn that just about anyone can still see for themselves in the mundane world is the one fixed in the heavens – the Unicorn Constellation.

The Unicorn or Monoceros constellation lies just to the left of Orion with his bright belt and between the constellations Canis Major (which contains the Dog Star Sirius) and Canis Minor; below Gemini on the ecliptic. The Milky Way runs right through it.

It is not always visible, depending on your latitude and the time of year, but in the northern hemisphere in mid-winter when you can see Orion's Belt clearly above the horizon, you should also be able to see most of the celestial unicorn to the left. It is a ghostly constellation though, with all its stars dimmer than fourth magnitude.

The constellation does however have one remarkable astronomical feature – a triple star system known as Beta Monocerotis discovered by William Herschel in 1781 and described by him as 'one of the most beautiful sights in the heavens'.

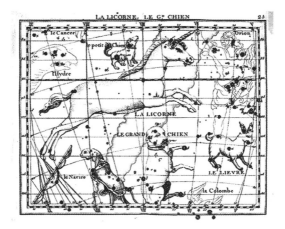

THE VISIONARY UNICORN

The unicorn has come a long way from the hazy rumours that Cstesias picked up in ancient Persia. In the Classical world it remained a curiosity on the sidelines, as it largely did in the countries it was supposed to inhabit. It was over a millennium later in Medieval Europe that the idea of the famous white unicorn truly flourished, sublimating or distilling all the story's components into the proud, graceful, shining creature of imagination we think of today, gracefully beckoning the way forward into the forest of idealistic possibilities.

In art and imagination the unicorn is no less inspiring than it was when people fervently believed in its physical reality. When a unicorn appears in pictures or stories its significance needs no explanation. Like angels and the Holy Grail, the unicorn has a clear place in our spiritual vocabulary, both to friends and foes.

Because there are foes – people whose instinctive reaction is mockery. A quite common saying in the United States is to describe something as being 'as likely as a sighting of a unicorn'.

On the other hand there are many unicorn enthusiasts who have no expectation at all of ever meeting one in the flesh, but whose fervour is completely undimmed. They even go on unicorn hunts and share their sightings of unicorns in the form of statues, paintings, shop signs, brand names and so on.

Among some fringe Christian groups it is believed that the new Messiah will come as a unicorn. Or at least that his return will be prophetically signalled by one, thanks to the mention of a beast with a single horn having many eyes in *Revelation*. Confusingly, the Antichrist may apparently take the same form. Telling one from the other will presumably be the test, if and when it happens.

From a quite opposite perspective, an interesting departure of the 1990s (largely on the internet, and still flourishing) is the cult of the Invisible Pink Unicorn, which is at least in part a philosophical tool for examining the nature of religious faith from a sceptical point of view. The satire is that while many of its tenets are patently absurd, if you substitute the word 'God' for 'Invisible Pink Unicorn' in its creed and revelations they often look uncomfortably like the piously held articles of faith of some major established religions that govern the very real behaviour of millions of people in the real world.

For example:

> *The Invisible Pink Unicorn is a being of great spiritual power. We know this because she is capable of being invisible and pink at the same time. Like all religions, the Faith of the Invisible Pink Unicorn is based upon both logic and faith. We have faith that she is pink; we logically know that she is invisible because we can't see her.*

Much more commonly though it is idealists and dreamers of a more perfect world who adopt the unicorn today, for much the same reasons as did the chivalric knights of old, blazoning it on their shields and banners and even adding a single horn to their steeds' head armour so that they resembled unicorns.

The pure white unicorn with its spiralling horn is a Platonic ideal, an archetype, and it was this that European travellers were really chasing through the wilds of Africa, India and America much more than natural creatures that simply happened, one way or another, to be single-horned.

It was like a search for the Holy Grail, a quest for possibly unattainable perfection, but a quest which seemed well worth pursuing anyway, just to prove that the everyday world is perhaps more magical than it often seems through the cold spectacles of pure materialism.

The true unicorn is a mystical creature endowed with wisdom and insight beyond the common human measure and able to communicate with the divine. Like an angel it can pass between worlds and dimensions.

One medieval legend says that although unicorns chose to accompany Adam and Eve in their expulsion from Eden, once a year they were allowed to return there to refresh their spirits – because it had been their free choice to enter the mundane world, it had not been forced upon them. The message of the legend is that the unicorn never was a completely flesh and blood creature; it always still partly belonged to Paradise.

FURTHER READING:

Beer, Rüdiger Robert *Unicorn: Myth and Reality*
1977, J.J. Kerry Inc

Bestiary: Translation of MS Bodley 764 Bodleian Library, Oxford
1992, Folio Society

Chevalier, Tracey *The Lady and the Unicorn*
2003, HarperCollins

Eschenbach, *Wolfram von Parzival*
1991, Continuum Publishing Co

Gould, Charles *Mythical Monsters*
1886, 1989 Bracken Books

Guerber, H A *Legends of the Middle Ages*
1909, 1993 Dover Publications
Online version: http://pge.rastko.net/etext/12455

Jung, Carl Gustav *Psychology & Alchemy: Collected Works Vol 12*
Routeledge, Kegan & Paul

Ley, Willy *The Lungfish, the Dodo and the Unicorn*
1949, Viking Press

Lum, Peter *Fabulous Beasts*
1951, Pantheon Books Inc

Shepard, Odell *The Lore of the Unicorn*
1930, 1994 Dover Publications
Online version: www.unicorngarden.com/shepard